The Pumpkin Mystery

by **Carol Wallace**

illustrated by

Steve Björkman

Holiday House / New York

To Keegan Keith Wallace
C. W.

For Sonora and Shad
S. B.

Reading level: 2.6

Text copyright © 2010 by Carol Wallace
Illustrations copyright © 2010 by Steve Björkman
All Rights Reserved
HOLIDAY HOUSE is registered in the U.S. Patent and Trademark Office.
Printed and Bound in April 2010 at Tien Wah Press,
Johor Bahru, Jobor, Malaysia.
www.holidayhouse.com
First Edition
1 3 5 7 9 10 8 6 4 2

Library of Congress Cataloging-in-Publication Data
Wallace, Carol, 1948-
The pumpkin mystery / by Carol Wallace ; illustrated by Steve Björkman. — 1st ed.
p. cm.
Summary: Two sleuths, a farm cat and dog, team up
with their enemy, a rabbit, to solve a Halloween mystery.
ISBN 978-0-8234-2219-7 (hardcover)
[1. Farm life—Fiction. 2. Domestic animals—Fiction.
3. Pumpkin—Fiction. 4. Halloween—Fiction.
5. Mystery and detective stories.]
I. Björkman, Steve, ill. II. Title.
PZ7.W15475Pu 2010
[E] —dc22
2009049148

Contents

Chapter 1

Too Early for Pumpkins

"What's going on out there, Mocha?"
asked Scruffy.
The cat rubbed against Mocha.
The two friends watched
through the fence.
Daddy opened the gate.
"Let's get the garden started,"
he said.

Scruffy's tail flipped as
he followed Mocha.
"Are you ready to get to work?"
Daddy asked Aden and Leah.
"Dad, can we plant pumpkins again?"

"Sure, but it's a little early,"
  said Daddy.
"Do you want them
  for Halloween?"
"Yes!" Leah and Aden shouted.
"Pumpkins take about 120 days
  to grow," Dad said.
"We need to wait until June."

"It was fun throwing the leftover
   pumpkins into the pasture."
   Aden smiled.
"You and your pals made a
   huge mess," Mama said.

Mocha rubbed her head
   against Aden's hand.
"We need to get the ground ready
   for beans and corn today," said Dad.
"Hey, where are the stakes?"
   Mom called from the shed.

Mocha ran to the shed.

"Steak! I love steak."

She sniffed and sniffed.

"Do you smell steak?" Mocha asked.

"They didn't mean food,"
 Scruffy said.

"Mama is looking for wood things."

"Why?" Mocha perked her ears.

"First they put the stakes
 in the ground.
 Next they stretch string
 between them.
 Then they have
 a line to follow
 for planting."

"Come on, Mocha, you can help dig!"

Mama scooped up Scruffy.

She put him in the wheelbarrow.

Mama pushed the cat to the garden.

Daddy walked behind the noisy tiller.

Dirt rolled from the metal tines.

"Want to dig for gophers?"

Scruffy invited.

"No thanks, I want to dig in
this nice, soft dirt."

The more Dad tilled the ground,
the more Mocha dug.

Dirt flew.

"Mocha! Stop digging!"

Daddy finally ordered.

"But this is fun," Mocha said.

"Mocha!" Daddy shouted again.

Chapter 2

Keep the Rabbits Out!

Daddy and Mama raked the dirt.

Aden and Leah counted the stakes.

Daddy pounded stakes
into the ground.

Mama stretched the string.

"It looks good!"

They all piled the soil
along the string.

Daddy and Mama poked holes
in the ridge of dirt.
Aden and Leah dropped seeds
in each hole.

Finally, Daddy covered
the seeds with soil.
Mama pulled the water hose
from the yard.
"Aden! Leah! Come water
the garden."

"So, what do we do next?"
Aden asked.

"We have to keep the weeds out,"
Mama said.

"Mocha will keep the rabbits out,"
said Daddy.

Mocha's ears perked. "I love to
chase rabbits."

When the tiny plants began to grow,
the rabbits started visiting
the garden.

"Stay away," Mocha growled.
"You're behind the fence.
You can't get us, Mocha Dog,"
said the rabbits.
Louie Rabbit nibbled
the tender plants.
Mocha barked and barked.

"Need some help, Mocha?"
Scruffy meowed.
The cat jumped from the tree.
"Run, rabbits," Scruffy said.
The rabbits ran from the garden.
Mama and Daddy worked
in the garden every day.

Aden and Leah watered
the seedlings.
Warm days brought more and
more tiny plants.
The beans in the garden
were up to Aden's knees.
The corn was higher
than Daddy's waist.

"Is it time to plant pumpkins yet?"
Aden asked.

"Sure, we'll soak the seeds in water.
That will give them a head start,"
Dad said.

Dad was up early working
on the tiller.
Aden pulled some big weeds.
Mocha and Scruffy sniffed the field.
The rabbits hid.

"We have to pile the dirt up," Dad said.
"We put five or six seeds
  in each mound."
Mocha started digging.
Aden and Leah piled dirt
to make little hills.
Daddy followed behind them.

He dropped seeds in the mounds.

Mama put dirt over them.

Mocha and Scruffy sniffed

the edge of the field.

"We'll let nature work," Daddy said.

Chapter 3

Where Are the Pumpkins?

"Are there any pumpkins?"

Leah asked.

"We *should* have some sprouts."

Daddy knelt down and dug

in the soil.

"Seeds are still here. No sprouts yet,"

Daddy said.

"Maybe they need more water."

Aden watered each mound.
"We may have to replant
the pumpkins.
The rest of the garden looks great."

A few weeks later
Mocha and Scruffy
followed Daddy and Mama.
Daddy stared at
the garden.

"What's happening to
our pumpkins?
We only have a few plants."
Mama put her hands on her hips.
"There are even fewer blossoms."
"It just doesn't make sense,"
Daddy said.

"I wanted another pumpkin party,"
Aden said.
"Everyone had a pumpkin
to decorate."

"I was going
to make a
princess one,"
Leah whined.
"We can **buy**
some pumpkins,"
Daddy said.
"It was fun to
have our friends
pick their own from the garden.
That was the best part," Leah said.
Aden sat down.
"The pumpkin
toss was the
best part,"
he said.

The leaves were beginning
to turn their fall colors.
Scruffy spotted Mocha
in her doghouse.
"Mocha, why are you moping?"
Scruffy asked.
"Leah and Aden are sad.
I wish they had some pumpkins.

Where are the pumpkins?"
Mocha whined.

"I just saw two pumpkins,"
Scruffy said.

"There are only five plants, and
the pumpkins are too small
and too green," said Mocha.

"The Mouse family got them,"
a quiet voice said.

"Who said that?" Mocha yipped.

"I've got some information for you."
The dog jumped up.

Louie Rabbit was standing
by the fence.

Mocha stepped closer.

"The rain washed some of
the seeds away.

Most of the others rotted.

There was too much water."

"How do you know?" Scruffy asked.

"Robbie, the baby mouse, told me.

He said his dad ate some
and got sick.

I can help you with your problem,
but we have to make a deal."
Scruffy and Mocha stared
at each other.
"What kind of deal?" Mocha asked.
"If you're looking for pumpkins,
meet me by the pecan tree in
the pasture."
The rabbit ran toward the barn.

Chapter 4

The Surprise

"Start barking. Mama will let
you out," said Scruffy.
Mocha barked and barked.
Mama came to the door.
"You need a run, Mocha?"
As soon as Mama opened the gate,
Mocha ran to the big tree.
Scruffy trotted behind him.

Louie was nibbling grass.
"We need to talk first," he said.

"What is it?" Scruffy asked.
"When your family starts
planting the garden in the spring,
we need some garden time."

"My job is to keep rabbits *out*!"
Mocha said.

"We don't want it all.
Your people plant a lot of seeds.
Then they thin out the rows.
We can take care of those
extra plants," Louie said.

"We can do that," Mocha yipped.

"Do you promise?" Louie asked.

"Yes," Scruffy and Mocha
said together.

"Okay. Follow me."
Mocha and Scruffy followed
Louie to the field.
"Look behind these bushes."
Louie scooted under the plant.
The dog and the cat shoved
through the bushes.
"Wow! How did you do this?"
Scruffy asked.
"I didn't do it. I just found it,"
Louie said.
"We'll be back!"
Mocha nudged
Scruffy.

When Mama opened the garden gate,
Mocha and Scruffy ran to the pasture.
Mocha barked as loud as she could.
"What's up with them?"
Daddy asked.

Aden ran after the dog and the cat.

"Mocha is barking at the bushes."

"Maybe it's an armadillo," Leah said.

"Or a skunk," Mama warned.

Mocha poked her nose
into the brush pile.
Scruffy shoved
his way into
the bushes.
"What is it?"
Aden asked.
Daddy pushed
back the limbs.

"Look at that!" Daddy said.
"PUMPKINS!" Mama, Aden,
  and Leah cried.

"How many do you see?"
  Daddy asked.
"One, four, seven, nineteen . . . ,"
  Leah counted.

Aden ran around the brush pile.
"MOM! DAD! There're tons
of pumpkins!"
"We can have our pumpkin party!"
Aden said.
"Where did these pumpkins
come from?"
Daddy scratched his head.

"We had the pumpkin toss here!"
said Aden.

"I guess we need to have
another pumpkin throw
in the pasture," Mama said.

"Mocha saved the day!"
Leah cheered.

Mocha and Scruffy looked behind
the clump of grass.

Louie was watching.

Scruffy purred.

Mocha wagged her tail.

Louie just wiggled his nose.